THE MOLE SI___
and the Wavy Wheat

Roslyn Schwartz

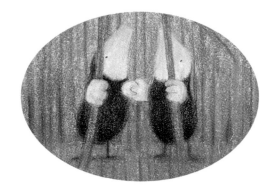

ZERO TO TEN

First published in Great Britain in 2005
by Zero To Ten,
part of Evans Publishing Group
2A Portman Mansions
Chiltern Street
London W1U 6NR

Originally published in North America by Annick Press Ltd.
© 2000 Roslyn Schwartz/Annick Press Ltd.
This edition © 2005 Zero To Ten Ltd

British Library Cataloguing in Publication Data
Schwartz, Roslyn
The mole sisters and the wavy wheat
1. Mole sisters (Fictitious characters) - Pictorial works - Juvenile fiction
2. Children's stories - Pictorial works
I. Title
813.5'4 [J]

ISBN 1 84089 385 0

Printed in China

To Stephanie and Carolyne

"Which way?"
said the mole sisters.

"We always go left..."

So they went right instead.

"Just for a change!"

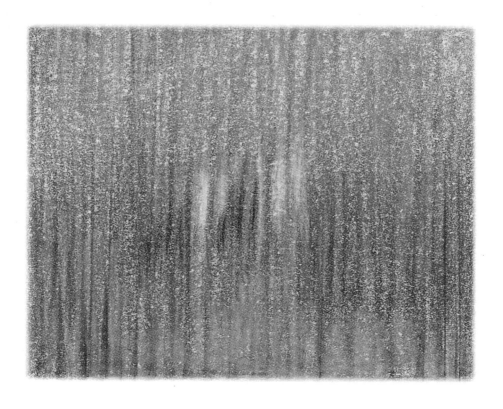

"Now which way?"
said the mole sisters.

"Hmmm —

UP!"

So up they went...

all the way to the top.

Oh dear.

"Yoo hoo!"

"YOO HOOOO!!"

"Let's go this way."

Oops.

"which way now?"
said the mole sisters.

"Yikes... hold on!"

swish to the right —

swish to the left —

one, two, three and...

"DOWN!"

The mole sisters waved
goodbye to the wavy wheat

and marched left right left right

all the way home.

Then they swept the mole hole
up down, up down.

"Now we've been
everywhere," they said.

"Everywhere except bed."

'Night 'night.

More books about the Mole Sisters:

The Mole Sisters and the Rainy Day
The Mole Sisters and the Fairy Ring
The Mole Sisters and the Moonlit Night